FATHER CHRISTMAS
AND THE DONKEY

Pikku Publishing
7 High Street
Barkway
Hertfordshire SG8 8EA

www.pikkupublishing.com

ISBN: 978-1-9996398-2-2

Text adapted and edited by Stephanie Stahl
Designed by Rachel Lawston

A CIP catalogue record for this book
is available from the British Library.

1 3 5 7 9 10 8 6 4 2

Printed and bound in China by Toppan Leefung Printing Ltd.

FATHER CHRISTMAS
AND THE DONKEY

Elizabeth Clark

Illustrated by

Ari Jokinen

Pikku Publishing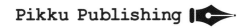

It was Christmas Eve, and the night was quiet and still. The stars and the little moon shone in the sky, and frost sparkled on the grass. It was a clear night, and it was very cold.

The old donkey, who lived on the common, was limping
along with his poorly leg towards a sheltered place.
It would be warmer there.

That Christmas Eve, the donkey was feeling very lonely. Even the brown cow that lived on the common had been taken back to her shed, full of warm straw and hay because tomorrow was Christmas Day.

The donkey had heard of Christmas, but he did not know much about it.

"Warm straw and hay," he said to himself, "Christmas must be comfortable!" The thought made the donkey feel hungry, but the grass was all stiff and frosted. It tickled his nose and then...

"Broo-oo-oof," he sneezed. He shook his head hard till his ears flapped, and brayed a long, mournful bray, "Ee-aw-ee-aw-ee-aw-ee-aw-aw-aw-aw!"

Down in the valley, the church clock began to strike twelve.
Each stroke sounded loud and clear in the stillness.
Then came another sound.

Somewhere up above, something went rushing by with a clear, sweet
ringing like silver bells, and a noise of faraway hooves galloping fast.

The donkey pricked up his ears and listened carefully. It made him feel as if he must gallop too. He could not remember galloping since he was a baby donkey. He was just going to try when he heard something coming up the hill.

The donkey waited and listened. He could hear footsteps crunching on the frosty grass. Then he saw somebody coming towards him – somebody in a long, red and white fur coat and big, fur-topped boots. He had a long, white beard and his eyes twinkled like two bright stars.

He was puffing a little. The sack on his shoulders seemed rather heavy.
He looked at the donkey and the donkey looked at him. There
seemed to be a wonderful, warm feeling all around.

"Happy Christmas, friend donkey," said a very kind voice.
"I heard you calling and you sounded lonely, so I came."

"I was lonely," said the donkey, "and I'm glad you
came, but may I ask, who are you?"

"Some people call me Father Christmas and some call me Santa Claus. It's all the same really."

"I remember now," said the donkey, "but where are your sleigh and reindeer?"

"I've sent them home tonight. It's after twelve o'clock," said Father Christmas. "Didn't you hear the sleigh bells go by?"

"Oh-h-h!" said the donkey. "So that was it."

"Yes," said Father Christmas, "that was it. The reindeer have been a long, long way tonight. We've been north, south, east and west – delivering presents to the world's children."

"There's only this last sackful to take
to Green Lane Hollow and a few places
on the way," said Father Christmas,
"but I can carry that myself."

The donkey looked at the sack.
It was large and it was bulging,
and it was certainly heavy.
"Green Lane Hollow is quite far
away," he said. "I could help
you carry the sack."

Father Christmas looked at the donkey
very affectionately and asked,
"But what about your leg?"

"I can manage," said the donkey stoutly.

Father Christmas laid the sack across the donkey's back, and they set off.
The sack was heavy, but the donkey's back was strong, and though
his poorly leg was stiff, it was wonderful how little it hurt.

On and on they journeyed. Sometimes the road dipped into
hollows where it was dark. Father Christmas would go ahead then,
to show the way. There was a kind of shining all around him.

But mostly Father Christmas walked beside the donkey with his hand resting on the donkey's shoulders. It gave the donkey a wonderful, happy warm glow to feel he wasn't alone.

Every now and again, they stopped to leave a parcel by the door of a house. As they reached the top of **Green Lane Hollow**, the donkey could feel that the sack was getting lighter.

Father Christmas looked up at the sky and nodded. "It's not long now **till daylight**," he said.

There was a pinky look in the sky as Father Christmas
and the donkey came to the bottom of the lane.
They stopped in front of a long, white cottage.

The house looked fast asleep, but then they
saw a little chink of light in a window, and
smoke began to fluff out of a chimney.

"That's Mrs Peterson," said Father Christmas.
"She's stirring up the fire. The house will be wide
awake in a moment. It's time for me to be going."

"Happy Christmas," said Father Christmas softly to the donkey, kissing him on his velvety nose. Father Christmas' tickly beard made the donkey want to sneeze. "Broo-oo-oof!" But the sneeze turned into a bray – a most tremendous bray!

"EE-aw-ee-aw-ee-awwwww," said the donkey. He heard someone give a little chuckle and he felt something touch his ears. He looked about, but Father Christmas was gone.

Now the cottage was awake – wide awake. The door flew open and there stood Mrs Peterson, looking surprised. Mr Peterson and three children were staring wide-eyed at the donkey from inside the house.

"Goodness me!" said Mrs Peterson. "Where did you come from?" Hanging from the donkey's ear was a neat little label that said, "I bring Happy Christmas to Green Lane Hollow!"

Mrs Peterson patted the donkey and gave him an apple to eat. Then she took the sack from his back, went inside, and emptied it out on the floor.

There was a football, a train and a doll for the children, a woollen coat for Mrs Peterson and a knitted waistcoat for Mr Peterson. There was a plum pudding in a basket and a box of sweets. So many presents!

The children patted and petted the donkey, and fed him some hay. They thought he was the best present of all.

That was Christmas Day, and the donkey has been at Green Lane Hollow ever since. He has grown quite sleek, and Mr Peterson has treated his poorly leg. The children enjoy playing with him, and when they are not in school, they can be found riding on his back!

He is truly a happy and contented old donkey!

I bring Happy Christmas to Green Lane Hollow!